A Turtle's Tale

MARIGOLD PRESS BOOKS

A division of International School of Story

A Turtle's Tale

Dr. Rose M. Metts

4

Characters

Mighty Maker: the Creator of all things and creatures
Gandophus: wise old turtle, overseer of the turtle population
Ralsh and Petail: young turtles, a brother and sister
Pashelo and Mishella: the turtle parents of Ralsh and Petail
Krazion and Samill: young turtle brothers
Katzio and Ziplota: the turtle parents of Krazion and Samill
Wismun and Folshelt: assistants to Gandophus
Flegal: Heron friend of Gandophus
Cratstofee: father of Gandophus

Places, Things, and Other "Creatures"

The River: a long canal flowing along a residential area
Grindmunchin: machines used in the canal renovation
Crushgroman: construction workers
Turkils: human beings
Silent Creatures: trash in the canal
The Ridge: a small holding pond with an aerator
Faraway Lake: a holding pond further away from the canal
Gindlemons: automobiles
Hard Ledge: a bridge over the canal for pedestrians and traffic

Table of Contents

Reader Reviews

"A delightful read for the life-long learner!" *Cindy Popejoy, home school parent*

"Dr. Metts' story about a turtle community is sweet (especially the conversations among the turtles) but also teaches about some behaviors of these interesting creatures God made." *Susan Ellis, wife of a retired pastor*

"This story . . . showed me a new perspective when looking at human behavior and the effects it has on nature and all of God's creatures. It is a lovely story that comes alive when the characters interact with each other." *Mary Ann Hogan, retired elementary teacher*

"A Turtle's Tale is an excellent story that illustrates the power of history, memory, and community. As they experience an unexpected disruption to their habitat, Metts' anthropomorphic turtles wrestle with issues common to humans, such as relationship dynamics, generational differences, and environmental change." *Dr. Chante Baker Martin, Educator*

Foreword

Growing up, I had several encounters with nature through playing outside, being a part of Girl Scouts, and going on family camping trips—with a real tent and poles! I had a great childhood.

Naturally, my fascination reached even to the turtles in a canal that I regularly passed. At one point, a catastrophic event was occurring in that waterway. A story was building up in my brain, and when I yielded to its prompting, this book was born.

As a side note, all injuries related to the turtles mentioned in this story are figments of my imagination, none were observed.

Acknowledgment

Many thanks to Dr. Chante Martin who was instrumental in helping my articulation of this fictional adventure.

A Turkil Ponders

Occasionally, workers cleaned out a particular canal containing a turtle population. My concern arose for the creatures' safety. One day, I asked one worker whether their work harmed the turtles, and he responded with a shrug.

Therefore, when a longer dredging occurred, in fact, major renovation of the canal, including the destruction of an overpass bridge, I wondered how this shelled population would feel. And how would this worker feel if he was the recipient of mechanical danger . . .

Glory Days

The bright ball in the sky poured its rays from above as Ralsh, his younger sister Petail, and their friend Tutker, stretched their heads out of their shells, then tucked their back legs inside again. It felt so good to sit together on the rocky ledge slightly above the water.

Ahhh. This is the life.

The area they lived in had a few rocks for resting, slopes for sunbathing, and a ridge that divided a smaller area of water from the larger river. Over the ridge, they could see a water spring and a smaller creek alongside a large structure where turkils gathered. Not many turtles lived over the ridge. It was too small and too close to the larger creatures.

Every now and then, closer to their habitat, several of the large turkils walked across the hard ledge above the turtles' home. The turkil creatures were tall and multi-colored, so different from the turtles. At times, one or two turkils would pass above them on the hard ledge, stop, and look down to observe them. Some turkils emitted guttural sounds, while others dropped items into the river.

Turtle parents constantly warned their youngsters about the turkils, short for "turtle-killers." Mishella cautioned her son Ralsh.

"Anytime you spot a turkil, get underwater—quick!"

"Why?" Ralsh questioned.

"They are dangerous, that's why! Some have thrown rocks at us. One even moved down the riverside to capture one of us! My father told me about a captive taken away from here and made to live in a square contraption and eat strange food. He died because they took him away from the water!"

With his mother's words echoing in his mind, Ralsh suddenly looked up. There was a turkil on the hard ledge, looking down on him and his companions. He didn't know if this turkil would harm him, but he wasn't going to hang around and find out. Ralsh submerged, dragging Petail with him, and Tutker quickly followed suit.

In their watery abode, they were invisible to the intruder. They could open their eyes underwater and see the turkil above. Turkils usually never dared to approach the water, and this one eventually wandered away.

"Hmmph!" grunted Ralsh. "Well, we are safe for now."

When the ledge was empty, the three youngsters returned to their favorite place on the rocks to bathe in the heat of the yellow ball high in the blue above.

There was a tunnel far below the ledge. It was not exactly pretty, but it sufficed. It was part of the home Ralsh had always known. Heavenly water flooded through the tunnel on cloudy days.

Suddenly, there was a splash nearby. Disturbed from their resting spot, the young turtles prepared to plunge into the safety of the water. But it was only Krazion, a brash young turtle, trying to scare them.

"Bug off, you!" yelled Tutker.

"This isn't your private domain! Anyone can come here!" retorted Krazion.

"Oh, leave him alone," sighed Ralsh.

Krazion poked Petail in her tail, and Ralsh rushed to her defense.

"Cut it out, Krazion!" he spluttered.

Ralsh nudged Petail away from Krazion and signaled to Tutker to move to a different location. They swam away from the upstart, with Ralsh in the lead and Petail and Tutker following.

"Ah, y'all think you're so smart!" snarled Krazion as the three moved away to a farther part of the river. Krazion continued his jeers.

"What a jerk," said Tutker.

The three friends clambered onto a new set of rocks to continue enjoying the warmth and light from above.

Every now and then, Ralsh caught a cricket and shared it with Petail. Tutker snapped a delectable plant for a snack. Then they swam around different parts of the river, being careful to avoid any turkils.

They watched as another turkil slowly moved along the ledge, looking down at them. It looked like the turkil they hid from before. Why was it here again? It held something up to the side of its head. What was that in its upper leg?

Ralsh wondered, What if the turkil tried to capture him and his friends this time?

"Quick! Hide!" Ralsh urged as he and Tutker dove down into the water.

Petail stayed afloat a bit longer, looking at the turkil. She sensed it was not an ordinary turkil. No, she felt a kinship with it. It felt more like a friend. She decided to rename it a "tur-kin."

Under the water, Ralsh steadily tapped at Petail's leg. When she didn't move, he resorted to using his mouth to pinch her tail. The pain reminded her to plunge beneath the murky water of their river.

After the turkil departed, Ralsh scolded his sister.

"Whatsamatter with you? Don't you know that those creatures are dangerous?"

Petail bent her head and followed her brother. However, she thought to herself, "I don't think that turkil was trying to hurt us. No, it's not a turkil. It's a tur-kin." She wanted to remember the tall creature for some reason.

Eventually, Ralsh and Petail heard their mom, Mishella, calling them to their nightly abode.

"Ralsh! Petail! Time to come home!"

"Awwww," Ralsh sighed. "Hey, Tutker, I'll see you tomorrow."

"Sure," replied Tutker as he headed toward his family.

Ralsh and Petail finally arrived in their section of the river where their parents waited. Pashelo, their father, reminded them it was time to prepare for colder weather.

"We've picked out the places for our winter home. Come over here and see the spots."

The four turtles swam over to the mud holes that Pashelo had prepared. They seemed to be the right size for each of them. Ralsh swam down and settled into his cozy spot. It was just right!

Petail grinned as she tested her space.

"Thank you! We love our spots!" they exclaimed. Both youngsters were thankful for such a considerate father.

When Ralsh and Petail were younger, they learned that as the weather became colder, each turtle would bury himself or herself deep within the mud. The Mighty Maker gave them the ability to breathe under the water from their warm dens. Then, as the outside air changed and warmed, they would swim up to the surface of the water and breathe normally.

Ralsh, being slightly older than Petail, remembered when the turkils damaged some of the turtles' wintering spots. Five or six turkils brought grindmuchins and disturbed the turtles' placid waters. Every one of the reptiles was forced to crawl or swim to a safe dwelling on the other side of the ridge. A few perished in the fray.

Krazion was almost smashed by a grindmuchin. On a personal dare, he waited until the metal claw nearly grazed his back. He practically leaped out of the way, laughing and yelling, "Ha, ha! You thought you got me that time! Geronimo!" He plopped into the river.

Ralsh shook his head remembering Krazion's strange behavior. "What a nut! I don't understand Krazion's dangerous ways."

Gandophus
The Teacher-Leader

Their ancient leader and teacher, Gandophus, had resided in the river for as long as Mishella and her husband Pashelo could remember. Every six days, the turtle community met together to hear what the elder had to say about the Mighty Maker.

Mighty Maker made each turtle with special characteristics to live underwater, especially during the cold spells. The way they breathed through different parts of their bodies was a gift from Mighty Maker. Their shells, which protected them from danger, were another gift.

Gandophus had two helpers, Wismun and Folshelt. The two young elders met with each enshelled family to provide support and comfort as needed. They also enforced rules to keep order. They visited troubled families and advised them during conflict and sorrow, and there were definitely some troubled families.

Krazion lived in a troubled environment. He and his mother, Katzio, were considered misfits in the turtle community. Katzio constantly complained about living in such a small area.

"You know this river isn't big enough for all of us!" she complained to Wismun one day. "In fact, I'd rather join my husband. You know, he lives abroad in a lake—so much bigger than this puny river!"

She neglected to mention the true reason her husband, Zioplas, lived away from his wife and son. Zioplas had left the family due to Katzio's aggravating behavior. She was always complaining and making discouraging remarks.

"These crickets are puny! What took you so long to come home?"

Wismun patiently listened, then reminded her that as a part of the community, she needed to be thankful for the good things. "Mighty Maker sees and hears all things," he reminded her. She would shut her mouth for a while and try to think about the blessings all around her. But a few days later, she'd commence her grievances.

All Krazion had now was his mother. She wasn't the best example for him, and his efforts at fitting in always seemed to fail.

Gandophus always warned the turtle community before the grindmuchins arrived. He seemed to have their schedule memorized. A partnership with Flegal, a heron friend, assisted Gandophus in his endeavor to prepare for the turkils and their monsters. Flegal was a feathered and faithful advisor. He not only regularly flew over their river but also flew for several miles on either side of it.

When Flegal spotted the crushgromen with their ugly yellow upper skins, he alerted Gandophus with a terse statement.

"They are here again. Expect noise. Tell the turtles to go into hiding."

Gandophus, in turn, called for an assembly to warn his shelled family to take cover. Wismun and Folshelt, his trusted advisors, usually assisted in rounding up the green amphibians.

Obediently, they waddled up the incline over the ridge and then took to whatever abode they could find. The tight quarters lasted only a day, so the population experienced few conflicts.

While all the turtles obeyed Gandophus's warnings each time, Krazion and Katzio always waited until the last minute to move to safety.

At first, the community fretted about their welfare with comments like, "Why do they always look for danger?" and "Those stupid folk!" After their third trip trooping over the ridge for safety, the turtle community began to ignore the dysfunctional pair.

A Turtle's Tale

Flegal and Gandophus

Strange Beings

Another of Gandophus's cautions regarded the silent creatures that occupied their river. These creatures never spoke or interacted in any manner. They never submerged, but instead always floated half on top of the river.

One creature was a large square, half-filled with water. Other cylinder-type creatures, some with flat sides, others with crooked rims, bobbed up and down. Turkils carelessly tossed these creatures on the ridge, and the skywater carried them down to the river through the tunnel. A few of the creatures had small openings, like a mouth, big enough to fit one's head in.

Gandophus warned the turtles, "Do not approach these silent beings. Many of them cause instant death."

A baby turtle, Samill, Krazion's little brother, had ignored the warning, much to his peril. Samill had spotted a minnow swimming inside one of the silent creatures.

"Oh, yum!" he said as he poked his head into the hole. He opened his mouth to enjoy the morsel, chewing it contentedly. Preparing to boast about his success to his brother Krazion, Samill discovered that he could not remove his head.

"Help!" he spluttered. His feet and tail thrashed as he struggled to set himself free.

Krazion swam to him.

"Hey! What happened? What's going on?"

In his effort to free Samill's head, Krazion's legs proved ineffective in pulling Samill away. Samill was drowning! Krazion helplessly watched his brother lose consciousness and float aimlessly, still trapped in the creature's mouth.

Katzio, their irate mother, fussed at Krazion for a week, spitting out the same words over and over again.

"Why didn't you keep an eye on Samill? What's wrong with you? You are a terrible brother!"

Zioplas, the boy's father and Katzio's husband, departed with a promise of some delicious minnows that evening. He never returned.

Maybe that's why Krazion always flirted with danger—not enough for his demise, but enough to scare everyone else.

A Troubling Speech

"Quickly, let's go! There is a message today!" The news spread among the turtle community that morning. Gandophus had something to say.

Pashelo nudged his children again and again. "Wake up! There's a special meeting!"

Ralsh shook his head to remove the drowsiness from his eyes.

"What was the hurry?" He murmured to himself,

They had eaten a good meal the day before, so they didn't need to eat. A message? What kind of a message was so important that they had to gather immediately? Ralsh pondered all of these things as they all made their way to the end of the ridge.

They carefully paddled with only their heads above water. They moved past the older turtles who were resting on the grassy slope next to the river. As they edged closer, Ralsh spotted the wrinkled figure, much larger than the crowd of shelled reptiles gathered around him.

"Oh, it's Gandophus." Ralsh said to his sister Petail. "He always warns us about the turkils and the grindmuchins. Yeah, yeah. We know about those things, and we've mostly been safe when those twin monsters came. What's so special about today?"

Flanked by Wismun and Folshelt, the dignified figure of Gandophus loomed above the crowd. He lifted his head, and the crowd became quiet, awaiting his message.

In a quivery voice, he said, "Bad days are coming! The turkils will be here for a longer span than usual. They will bring huge grindmuchins, more than the usual number. They will tear down our protective ledge and close our river. We must prepare by going over the ridge for safety. Beware! Do not stay here! Beware! We must leave our home!"

The younger turtles stared in amazement, the parents looked stern, and the teens rustled restlessly. They had to leave their placid river? To move away from the rocks of rest? Would there be enough room for them all in the smaller water?

Krazion started to mutter, "Crazy old man! We already know . . ." but his mother, Katzio, cut him off.

"Quiet down! This is serious!"

A few hundred feet away, Ralsh grinned in Krazion's direction. Krazion snarled at him but said nothing.

Gandophus continued with more warnings and suggestions for safety. "You must move over the ridge to the smaller water. It will be uncomfortable, but it will not last long. Everyone must move in the next few days. I have appointed Wismun and Folshelt to assist with the relocation."

Gandophus then trudged down the ridge on the other side. His movement gained everyone's attention. He usually slid down into the water and swam to the far side to a quiet place away from everyone else.

For Gandophus to travel over the ridge already must mean it is a truly dangerous time for all. No one wanted to move, to uproot. They always carried their shelters with them and could withdraw at any time and remain unseen—their shells closing the door behind their bodies. However, it didn't look like the protection of their shells was going to be enough this time.

As the reptiles left for their homes, they each had to decide how to proceed, and when to proceed in following Gandophus. Each father turtle decided to waddle ahead and scope out a possible new location for his family. Mothers fretted over the special marks they made in their present homes. Young turtles whined about the loss of their play areas. They were all sad to leave.

Two groups of turtles immediately heeded Gandophus's warning. They covered over their mud holes, gathered up their young, and made the long trek over the ridge to the smaller pool with the water spring. Two more families joined them. The smaller area was already getting crowded, but at least they would be safe.

The other turtles who stayed behind thought that perhaps they had more time to make the move. In the meantime, they thought, "Let's stay put. We'll have time to make it out of danger. We have always survived before. We will survive again."

A Turtle's Tale

A Prophecy Fulfilled

Ralsh pondered everything as they swam to their newly formed holes—the ones his father made for the winter. Would they even get to spend one more night? Maybe not. His parents would decide.

Ralsh chatted with Tutker. "Whatta ya think? Will there be more danger?"

"I don't know," Tutker replied. "But Gandophus has never been wrong. Each time, his message came to pass."

"Hmmm," mused Ralsh. They said no more about the impending danger and went back to playing.

A few weeks later, the cold air came. All the remaining turtles swam to their winter holes, settled in, and buried themselves in the mud.

One day, a slight noise stirred Mishella. She nudged Pashelo. "Something is wrong. I can feel it."

Pashelo replied, "You are a worry-wart. The kids are fine. We need to sleep to be ready for the warmer air."

"No. Something's wrong. I heard a funny noise above the waters."

"Now, look here . . ." Pashelo began to chide his wife, but then suddenly stopped. "Wait," he said, "I hear it too."

Suddenly, their home was trembling. Pashelo tucked into his shell. Surely, this was just the turkils with their regular routine.

Several roars pierced the air. Pashelo popped his head out of his shell, looked up, and saw their shadow-making ledge crack and crumble. Several yellow-jacketed turkils roamed along the edge of their river. Huge grindmuchins surrounded the ledge and a few came down the side of the river.

These monsters were tearing away at the resting rocks and plunging into the water. The roaring and cracking grew louder and louder.

"The prophecy of Gandophus!" shouted Mishella. "We must flee!"

Frightened, the turtles who had remained in the river scampered out of the water. Tiny infants clung to the backs of their parents or other adults as they crawled over the ridge. Krazion scrambled with his mother, his confused face matching that of the other fleeing turtles.

Ralsh looked behind him. One of the grindmuchins caught a couple of older turtles, sucking them in never to be seen again. Another grindmuchin flipped two smaller reptiles into the air with a big clump of mud. The crowd of fleeing turtles inched their way over the ridge.

Gandophus sat with Wismun and Folshelt on either side as they awaited his command. Flegal roosted on a tree close to the crowd.

Why was Flegal still here? The turtles mumbled to themselves. He usually stayed only a day or two after alerting their leader.

As if to satisfy the curiosity, Gandophus explained, "As I said earlier, the turkils will work for a very long time. Flegal will watch for us, flying over the danger and alerting us to the progress. In the meantime, find cold-weather shelters where you can. I know it will be crowded, but it can be done. Let's share space amiably."

Gandophus arranged a monthly gathering to keep his harried horde abreast of the progress. He decided to slowly disperse any "good news" of the return to normalcy. He also directed his two trusted advisors to select assistants to watch over the turtles and keep them out of danger. Wismun and Folshelt recruited four extra turtles to guard the ridge's downslope. They would also report on the dangerous work going on in the river.

"We might need to enforce the Shell Code," Folshelt advised. "I know you dislike punishing our people, but we must think of safety. . ."

Gandolphus shuddered. He remembered past experiences of the Shell Code. When he was a young adult turtle, he helped his father, Crafstofee, build a small enclosure of leaves with a slight opening in the front. It was an area they would use to punish offenders of the Shell Code.

"What is this for?" young Gandolphus asked his father.

"The Maker instructed me to do this. He knows that not all of our population will obey our instructions. We must keep our turtles safe," Crafstofee taught his son about the community rules, to be kind, do justly, and act humbly.

Anyone who broke the Shell Code was pushed into the enclosure and given only enough water and food to keep him or her alive. No one, not even family members, could visit that place. Other turtles were prohibited from talking to the banished turtles.

Sure enough, a terrible experience occurred five months after Gandolphus's father built the enclosure. Some of the shelled reptiles had formed a group of males that stole food from families and bullied youngsters. Young Gandolphus and two new apprentices, Wismun, and Folshelt, constructed four new enclosures, enough for each offender.

The reptiles remained in the enclosures until they accepted a pledge to either obey the Code or leave the population. The oldest offender refused to conform, so Gandophus and his helpers led that turtle to the hard ledge and told him to leave the community.

Another male who refused to obey died from loneliness while locked in the grassy cave. The other males pledged to behave according to the simple community guidelines set down by the Maker.

It was a harsh memory, but one Gandophus knew served a purpose. After Crafstofee passed away, Gandophus wanted to avoid further tragedy. He modified the Shell Code so that each punishment would better fit the violation. And now, he would have to be prepared to enforce a Shell Code to protect the community at large.

Turtles on the river bank

The Problem

The turkils worked long days. They stopped the river from flowing and then created a new ledge of dirt for young turkils to travel. They redirected the water to a small pond beside the dirt ledge.

Flegal winged his way along the former path of the river and reported all the details to Gandophus. The elderly leader waited a few days before telling the information to his anxious population in their monthly gathering. Several cries arose from the shelled mass when he shared the news.

"What?! Our river is gone? Where will we live? How will we survive? What are they doing? Do they want us to die?"

Gandophus attempted to allay their fears. "The Maker told me our river will be restored, along with the heat-blocking ledge and rocks for resting. Do not fear. All will be made right."

The turtles still murmured among themselves. Some accused Gandophus of "rock dreams" while others doubted that the Maker spoke to their leader—or even if there was a Maker.

Discontent arose over two matters. First of all, the turtles had to establish new residences. Crowded in the smaller area, tensions arose over mud holes for winter. The earlier arrivals—obedient to Gandophus's speech—had settled into the best places and refused to budge, always citing their privilege in those spaces for being first. The stronger males—husbands wanting the best for their families—fought with less aggressive males, flipping them over or ramming their shells, all to obtain a better space.

Gandophus stepped in often, biting the tail of both adversaries and designating their respective spaces. After a while, the crammed population settled in.

The other issue the community faced involved food. Without the spacious river and its abundance, the turtle families had to scrounge for their meals. Conflicts arose when turtles spotted the same morsels and wrangled for dominance.

Gandophus stepped in again, but in a different manner. "This matter of food is beyond my capacity. I must seek the Maker for provision."

Some scoffed behind his back, but the next few days before hibernation started, the turtle families discovered provision in areas where none had been the day before. Each turtle family found enough food to feed themselves and their young ones each day. "Just enough . . ." most marveled at this discovery. "Gandophus must have the mercy of the Maker indeed!" some remarked.

Not satisfied with sufficient nutrition, some turtles talked about moving to the Faraway Lake. Oblong rather than linear, it resembled the space like the ridge, with a rising spout of water. It would take several turtle days to travel to Faraway Lake, and who knew what the turkils would do to those who attempted the journey.

Grandparents told horror stories of their kin who died by moving gindlemons, whizzing over the hapless victims.

"My uncle walked onto the long hard path," stated an elder tortoise, "and a scarlet grindlemon ran over him! He looked like a flattened green block on the hard path!" Younger listeners shuddered at the mental vision.

"Ha!" bragged Krazion. "I can make that trip any day! Watch me!"

"Watch ME!" yelled his mother, who bit his tail. He stopped, sulking. Despite the intermittent talk of such an exploit, no one wanted to venture into the unknown.

Over the ridge, the turtle families eventually dug mud holes and settled in for the colder weather. Ralsh thought as he settled in, "We are—shell to shell— packed as tightly as sardines."

Sardines! He licked his mouth as he remembered hearing about that tasty snack. His mother told him about a silent creature floating in the river that once held sardines. She had tasted a sardine that floated out of the silent creature into her path. That was an interesting find in what used to be their river. What will the river be like in the warmer weather—who knows? There may not be a river or any silent creatures in their world ever again.

A Turtle's Tale

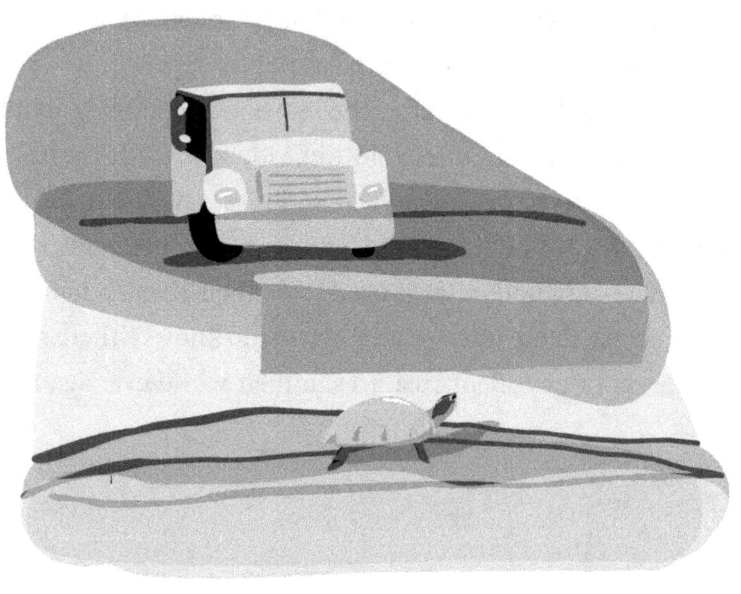

Cautious Optimism

The turtles slumbered in their winter mud holes for a long time. Then, slowly, gradually, the cold streams of air transformed into lukewarm breezes. The bare trees awakened, shooting forth tendrils of green. The grass slowly turned from brown to green. Though they did not see the transformation, the turtle population felt it. Still, just as a snake loathed departing from its warm underground den, so the shelled population lingered in their warm winter shelter.

Gandophus awoke from slumber, alert. He dispatched Flegal, "Review the area and report to me."

After an hour away, the feathered overseer returned, bringing news.

"The turkils seem to be rebuilding the hard ledge. The noise of the grindmunchins has dwindled because most of the larger grindmunchins have left the area. There aren't many left. Instead, the number is now down to two or three."

Gandophus aroused Wismun and Folshelt to check out the area as well. As commanded, the two advisors crept over the ridge look over the situation. They returned to Gandophus with excited voices.

"The river is being reconstructed with new rocks lining it. The hard ledge is being built again!"

Gandophus shushed them. "Do not let this news escape. If the turtles hear, they might return too soon. No, let's keep quiet for now. Please put a lockdown into place close to the top of the ridge. It should warn any straying turtles to stay on this side of the ridge."

"Lockdown" was a temporary fence of strong river weeds, built to enforce Shell Code. If it had a cover, it resembled the trap turkils used to catch the hapless sea creatures valued for their long, shelled arms with claws that pinched. Turkils called those creatures "crabs." Those deciding to leave the ridge against orders would be placed into lockdown. While there, they experienced the uncomfortable, choking feeling of being confined. Few, if any turtles in this population, wanted to be placed in lockdown.

Gandophus's warning to keep silent failed in one area. Krazion, who was never a sound sleeper, slowly emerged from his mud hole and spotted the excited face of Folshelt. Krazion heard neither the news of the new river nor what Gandophus had said. Nevertheless, he suspected something had happened. He decided to look at the river for himself but waited until nightfall.

At twilight, he crept up the hill of the ridge and had almost reached the top when Wismun, who was standing guard with Folshelt, stopped him.

"Where are you going, Krazion?"

"Uh . . . uh," stuttered Krazion.

"Get back down to your mother and stay away from here," warned Folshelt. "The grindmunchins will tear you to pieces. If you don't know how to listen, you will be sent to lockdown."

Sulkily, Krazion returned to his mud space. But a week later, Krazion attempted another look. In the early morning, he crept in another direction, taking a roundabout way to the former river. One of Folshelt's assistants was nodding at his guard post. Krazion slowly wriggled a good way away from the guard and climbed to the top of the ridge.

He made it! The huge ball in the sky had already risen midway between earth and the blue above. Yes! It was true! The river was being rebuilt and . . .

Whoom! A grindmuchin caught Krazion by one leg and swung him down. He writhed in pain and struggled to get away. A crushgroman saw the reptile and shouted something. Finally, the large claw of the grindmuchin opened and Krazion fell tail-first onto the bare ground. Stunned, he lay there for several minutes. Finally, he groaned and hobbled slowly to the ridge. His leg throbbed as he dragged it along.

Several of the turtles were rising from their mud holes in response to the warmer breezes. Ralsh, resting on the proper side of the ridge, spotted a familiar shape that moved strangely.

What? Was that Krazion with the distorted face? Yes, it was.

Wismun stood at his guard post but turned to see Krazion as well.

Ralsh spotted the torn limb of his former adversary. Asking Wismun's permission, Ralsh climbed to the top of the ridge to help.

He told Krazion to climb on his back and he would bring him back to his mother. Krazion gladly complied. They arrived back to his mother, and she couldn't believe her eyes. After expressing grief over his injuries, Katzio shrieked at Krazion's foolishness.

Enforcing the Shell Code was justified as Krazion had disobeyed. Wismun came to put Krazion in lockdown until he healed. Under

Gandophus's orders, female turtles would apply treatment to his leg.

Ralsh returned to his family and related the whole adventure.

"Well," said Pashelo. "You did what was right. I'm glad."

"So am I," replied Ralsh thoughtfully. "Maybe things will be different with Krazion in the future."

Krazion in lockdown

Return to Glory

The area on the other side of the ridge became peaceful once again. The sound of grindmuchins and the chatter of turkils decreased. The shelled population noticed the difference, wondering what such changes meant. They received an answer. Gandophus called another assembly.

The turtles squeezed into the area behind the ridge full of curiosity, excitement, and despair. When would they get more space? When would they return to their homes?

Gandophus started his announcement. "Flegal has reported the river is restored. The hard ledge that makes shadows is restored. The rocks are restored. You may move back to your former dwellings. Please make sure that you return to YOUR former dwellings. Wismun and Folshelt will ensure everyone follows these directives. Immediately after our return, meet me under the shadowing ledge."

The other turtles gleefully filed over the ridge to locate the dwelling areas they longed for. Slowly, the green and brown horde returned to their beloved river. Outbursts of pleasure and joy erupted during the trip.

"Look! Look at the rocks! They are so bright and clean!"

"Look at the river! Is it wider than before?"

"I am so glad to be back!"

"Wonderful!"

The assembled turtle folk met again under the ledge as directed, and Gandophus thanked the Maker for their return as well as for the improvements made in their former home. Mishella and Pashelo grinned at each other. They signaled to Ralsh and Petail to follow them to their new abode. They located the spot and settled in, as did the rest of the population. Confusion and noise turned into restful satisfaction for all.

The next morning, Ralsh and Tutker searched for their usual place of frolic. They swam around and then rested on the rocks. Krazion slowly paddled toward them, a little lopsided due to his injury. He looked at Ralsh shyly.

"Hey," he said.

"Hi," replied Ralsh.

"Um, just wanted to thank you for helping me a while back."

"Sure, glad to do it. So, what are you up to this morning?"

"Just wanted to hang out with you if that's okay."

"Yeah!"

What a relief not to encounter a surly face or sarcastic remarks. Ralsh, Krazion, and Tutker paddled over to some of the new large rocks and climbed up to settle there and bask in the sun. Petail followed, marveling at the new Krazion, his brazen attitude gone. Even his mother, Katzio, settled down and befriended Mishella.

Suddenly, the shadow of a turkil fell on the young turtles.

"Quick! Submerge!" ordered Ralsh.

Petail slowly descended, but stopped when she recognized the turkil. No, not a turkil—a turkin! She sensed happiness emanating from this being. The turkin was delighted the shelled population enjoyed their improved home. Petail kept her eyes on the turkin, even as she submerged below the water's surface.

A Word From the Turkin

The last truck had left the area. It was all quiet now. So much had changed. I stood on the new bridge over the canal, hoping the turtles survived the noise and confusion.

I left home early to survey the new canal, following my usual path. Arriving at the site, I spotted the new rocks placed in strategic areas in the renovated waterway. It looked wonderful!

The best part of the renovation was the line of turtles resting on the rocks. I counted them. There were ten of them! On the other side of the canal rested seven more turtles. Yes! They survived the turmoil!

I watched as four turtles floated close to the bridge. They quickly submerged—except for one, who moved more slowly than the other two.

I felt a kinship to that one, but didn't know why . . .

Dr. Rose M. Metts

Dr. Rose Metts was an associate professor of English at Savannah State University. She retired after teaching classes in English Composition and Literature for 26 years.

Her accomplishments include teaching study abroad courses to college students in China and directing several community ventures. One of the most notable programs she led was a literacy program that connected undergraduate volunteers with elementary schoolers in need of reading support. She also organized a composition and art event for youth at a local community center and, with her husband Dan Metts, launched a neighborhood Bible Club to mentor young people in their community.

Dr. Metts has presented material from her dissertation, "Rhetorical Strategies of the Inter-racial Church," at several regional conferences. In fact, as a professor, she always used those opportunities to encourage college students to participate in scholarly conferences by bringing them with her as co-presenters. Dr. Metts remains active in community initiatives that combine her passions for working with youth and promoting literacy.

MARIGOLD PRESS BOOKS

A division of International School of Story

www.ingramcontent.com/pod-product-compliance
Lightning Source LLC
Chambersburg PA
CBHW070512170726
48291CB00008B/2725